Freedom

Bethel Abiy

Ukiyoto Publishing

All global publishing rights are held by

Ukiyoto Publishing
2nd edition
Published in 2023

Content Copyright © Bethel Abiy
ISBN 9789359204994

www.ukiyoto.com

"Every good and perfect gift is from
above, coming down from the Father of the
heavenly lights, who does not change like
shifting shadows."

-    James 1:17

Dedication

I would like to start off my dedication by saying thank you to God, the true creator. Without Him, my book would not even exist. I would also love to appreciate my supportive family and friends. If it wasn't for them, I would have doubted my capabilities.

Acknowledgment

In this book, I extend my heartfelt acknowledgment to my family, and friends, with special gratitude towards my parents for their unwavering support throughout the publication of both editions of my book. My sister and friends gave me hope, instilling in me the belief that my words would one day find their way into the hands of readers, and their continued presence by my side has been a source of immense strength.

Additionally, I would like to extend my profound appreciation to two individuals who played crucial roles in the publication of the first edition of this book: Mr. Habtamu, the head counselor of my high school, and Mr. Ndaba, a literature teacher. For directing me to the path to reach my achievement.

I am forever grateful to each and every one of these remarkable individuals.

Contents

Bethel Abiy

Journey

Freedom

As Positive

As Negative

Freedom

Fighting

Image

Journey

Art

One

Word

World

Bethel Abiy

Art

Reading an art piece has more beauty
than what our eyes can ever let us see

As Positive As Negative

As much as I am positive, I can also be negative
As bright as the sun gets, it can also get dark
As fast as my heartbeats, it can also beat slow

As much as I love, I can also hate
As much as I am kind, I can also be rude
As much as I build up, I can also break down
As much as you trust me, I can also betray you
As much as I hold you, I can also let you go

As much as I laugh, I can also cry
As much as I am smart, I can also be dumb
As much as I speak, I can also be silent

Bethel Abiy

Freedom

*B*eauty has risen in strong ways
*E*ars hearing birds sing
*T*ongue tasting as much as kings
*H*air dancing with the wind
*E*yes watching the ocean breathe
*L*uxury freedom is all I have

Fighting

Time is flying
Sky is whining
Sun is shining
Courage is dying
My heart is lining
'Cause I am lying
Have to stop whining
And start fighting

Bethel Abiy

Image

A person is like an image
You can see them from far,
But all you see is their structure

As you get closer
You can see them more clearly
You will see their smile and scar
You will start to see the things that were hidden by
the distance

At the maximum point
You will see who they truly are

You see the details of their personality

Journey

*B*ring brightness to your life
*E*very day is a time to shine
*T*o be honest, the truth hurts
*H*ell is also found on earth
*E*vil can also be found from birth
*L*oyalty is my destiny for the journey

Bethel Abiy

One Word

One word has
A thousand meanings
A million feelings
A billion sightings

One word can
Give you pain
Give you peace
Or keep you the same

World

What have you done to me?
Over this past century

Remember all the love we had?
We were living for one another
But now you are living for your future
I give you warmings but you keep on destroying me
Don't forget we die together

I was created before you
Have control over your power
Shoot fire
flood
and even swallow you

Let us recreate what we had
Or
Regret what we could have had

Bethel Abiy

I gave you 21 years but you're still walking in your
own way

I will give you 11 days

To reverse the tragedy you created

Question

Bethel Abiy

Friend

MOON

Who Are You?

Education

Just Keep Quiet

YOU

Past

Present

Future

Protect

Education

I learn I learn
But what is the use
If I don't make a change
And learn from my mistake

Do I have books for the sake of learning?
Or to absorb and make a change to the existing

You should remember education is nothing
But a key to the world if you change something

Bethel Abiy

Friend

Friend friend friend
What is the meaning of a friend?
If they just go and come
And never stay with you till the end
They are not a shadow, they are a friend

Friend friend friend
Who is the friend?
If they just hate
And don't have faith

Friend friend friend
Are you my friend?
It is hard to say
`Cause you are in my way

Friend friend friend?

Just Keep Quiet

Just keep quiet if you want to learn something
Or keep talking if you are the one teaching

Just keep quiet and listen to the silence
Or keep talking and disturb your peace

Just keep quiet and listen to yourself
Or keep talking and ignore your thoughts

Just keep quiet and feel the music
Or keep singing and reflect on your feeling

Bethel Abiy

Moon

Looking out the window
While everything around is shallow

You're staring at me
But I don't know what to say
I wasn't looking for you
But you appeared

Not moving away
Not blinking
As if you're frozen

I feel the guilt
I feel the betrayal
As you speak through the night
But we all walk away as if we're blind

Past Present Future

Past present future
Where are you now?
Studying the past?
Living in your present?
Or dreaming about your future?

Where are you going to be tomorrow?
Regretting today?
Making the day?
Or walking your way?

You should stop dreaming
And start achieving
Because your future is coming
Your present is living
And your past is fading

Bethel Abiy

Just remember tomorrow will never come

It is just a word that doesn't exist
But today is the day when you can change your future

And yesterday has died just leave it alone and walk
away

Think about your future while living in the present
and leaving your past

Protect

You can't protect an egg from hatching
It's going to rotten instead

You can't hold a person from expressing
They're going to hurt inside instead

Bethel Abiy

Who Are You

You are running away, I can't catch you
You're my enemy that is why I'm trying to fight you
Why won't you stop for me because I need you
You are like the air; it is hard to keep you

I watch you go by, but I can't see you
You are the same every time, but different every day

You are ringing in life we can't stop you

What are you?
Where are you?
Who are you?

You

You
Everyone's common name
Doesn't have a special meaning
Just goes with everyone that's existing

You
Defined to express a person right there
Defined to express everyone

Bethel Abiy

Creation

Freedom

Future

Rising Sun Not

The Setting Moon

Quality

Is Better Than

Quantity

So Please Stop

Culture

Survive

Every

peace

Bethel Abiy

Culture

We see the world in different ways
We hear the beat through our veins
We feel the pattern that comes from our name

I say they're beautiful
But you think they're ugly
I feel the music
But you find it disturbing

Do you think culture is important?
`Cause we are losing it
My culture is my habitat
But they are destroying it

Years ago they were strong
But look at today they are drifting away

Freedom

If culture did not exist we would not have existed
Do not let it go

How would you define yourself without culture?
How would you express yourself without culture?

Bethel Abiy

Every

Every day I see you

Every week I greet you

Every year I cheer for you

Every decade I wrinkle cause of you

But a century is one in a million can see

Where do you go after that `cause I just hear about
you.

Freedom

Future

I see my future
Ahead of me
I see the path
That's guiding me

The
Red
Yellow
Green
Light

That's telling me
To walk slowly
Or cross the street

The journey is long
I see no endpoint
The line is endless
Made of head points

Bethel Abiy

Peace

May God bring you peace
All the pain
Anxiety
Nervousness
Depression
Burnout
Took time to get there
It will take time to leave

May God bring you peace
and take everything that you call pain away

Quality Is Better
Than Quantity

Quality,

a precious gem so rare,

Like a diamond, few have the chance to wear it.

A mark of distinction, a treasure to show

Quantity,

a vast ocean of creation,

Surpassing our population's

Endless numbers, expanding wide

We all love Quality but produce Quantity

Only the unique can create it, endlessly

Bethel Abiy

Rising Sun.
Not The Setting Moon

I don't see the world through their eyes
That is why I have my own
I have two ears and a mouth
That is why I listen more than I speak

I use me as a witness
That is why I like to fight alone

We are in a world
Where people fight as if there is no tomorrow
We are in a world in which we fight with three people
Me, Myself and I

Can you imagine where we would have got
If we all fought together as one

We would have been the rising sun and never see the
setting moon

Survive

Life goes on as we breathe

Time goes off as we live

Wishes appear from our dream

We see tears when it gets cold

We all study just to erase

We all believe in order to create

Give you my applause even for your mistake

I live in the day and die at night

But no matter what I am still surviving

Bethel Abiy

Reflection

What is **Freedom?**

____

____

____

____

____

____

____

About the Author

Bethel Abiy

 Bethel Abiy is a young author who was born in Ethiopia, she loves writing about different topics regarding life and is a creative and open-minded artist who cultivates her mind in the art of poetry.

Her previous work includes her debut book, Freedom, the first edition of this book. It was published in 2020 during her time in high school by Ukiyoto Publishing. Her work and story amazed readers, prompting her to publish a second edition as a result.

Bethel is currently embarking on much larger projects and eagerly working on her second book, Coming Soon!

To discover more about the author and her inspiring works, visit her website at www.betelbisrat.com